MY BROTHER IS A
ROBOT

BOOK 1

THE EXPERIMENT

AMANDA RONAN

The Experiment
My Brother is a Robot #1

Copyright © 2016

Published by Scobre Educational

Written by Amanda Ronan

Scobre Educational
2255 Calle Clara
La Jolla, CA 92037

Scobre Operations & Administration
42982 Osgood Road
Fremont, CA 94539

www.scobre.com
info@scobre.com

Scobre Educational publications may be purchased for educational, business, or sales promotional use.

Cover and layout design by Nicole Ramsay
Copyedited by Kristin Russo

ISBN: 978-1-62920-495-6 (Library Bound)
ISBN: 978-1-62920-494-9 (eBook)

For Christopher.

Always and forever, so so so much.

CHAPTER 1

I PUSHED PAST JAMES, GIVING HIM A TASTE OF MY ELBOW AS I curved my arm and took the shot. The ball sailed out of my hand, arced through the air and . . . missed the net. Again.

I sighed. "Man, my game is off today."

James howled from the free throw line, "My nana can do a better layup than that. And she's in a wheelchair." He doubled over with laugher.

The anger was starting to rise up into my throat, so I shoved the ball at James, hard. "If she's so great, then play with her tomorrow afternoon. I'm sick of this." I jogged down the street and up to the front of my house. My mom's car was in the driveway, which meant she was home early from work. Mom had a cool job at Smith and Company Engineering Laboratory—they did all kinds of high-tech stuff there.

"Oh, come on, bro!" I heard James call as I opened the front door. "I was just playing."

Well, tomorrow you'll play without me, I thought as I dropped my coat on the floor by the door.

"Shawn!" My father stood up from the couch. "What do you think you're doing?" Dad was a big man, with a big voice. Sometimes my mom joked that he was just a big teddy bear, but I thought of him more like a drill sergeant. He liked rules and order, rhyme and reason.

"Hey, Pops. I was just going to go do my homework." I gestured to my bedroom, which was upstairs.

He walked over to me, leaned down, and picked up my jacket. "What's this?"

"Oh yeah, my jacket. *That's* where I put it!" I laughed and reached for it.

My dad held on to the sleeve. "If I've told you once, I've told you a thousand times—"

Let me finish this for you with any number of things my father has nagged me about:

—*don't put your elbows on the table while we're eating.*

—*sit up straight.*

—*don't talk with your mouth full.*

—*don't be a slacker.*

—*don't slurp the milk out of the cereal bowl.*

—*gum should not be stuck on the bottom of the dining room chairs.*

—*no drawing moustaches on photos of your grandmother.*

"—pick up your stuff, I am not your maid."

"Yeah, got it, Dad," I rolled my eyes and hurried over to the stairs.

"And be ready for dinner in fifteen minutes. Your mother has something important to tell us."

As we ate dinner, my mom's foot bounced up and down under the table and she kept tapping her fork against her plate.

"Mom?" I asked, wondering what was going on.

"Are we done with dinner? That's great! I have something very exciting to show you!" She stood, dropping her fork onto the plate with a clink.

"No, we are not done, thank you very much. Shawn needs to finish his vegetables before he is excused from the table." Dad sat back in his chair with his arms crossed.

Mom looked from Dad to me to the cauliflower left on my plate. "Okay, well, you finish up. I'll go set up." She hurried out of the room.

Set up? I thought. *For what?*

"Samira!" Dad called and followed her out of the room.

I waited a beat and then took the time alone to scrape the cauliflower into the trashcan. Scooter, our chubby basset hound, whimpered at my feet as he saw food being deposited somewhere other than his belly.

"Shawn, come into my office! Bring Scooter!" Mom called.

I leaned over to scratch behind Scooter's ears and rub his belly. "Come on, lazy. Mom wants to show us something."

Scooter's ears perked up a little and he rolled onto his stubby little legs to follow me through the living room to Mom's secret laboratory.

Okay, it wasn't really a secret. Mom wasn't really an evil scientist, though I sometimes let the other kids in the neighborhood think that. It helped my street cred.

"What do you think it is this time, boy?" I asked Scooter. "Maybe a magical flying carpet?" Mom came home with so many wacky ideas it was hard to believe she had a Ph.D. in mechanical engineering.

I looked at Scooter, who tilted his head to one side. "No, you don't think so? Well maybe it's a talking dog collar. Would you like that, Scoot? Would you like us to know what you're really trying to say with all your grunts and whimpers?" Scooter hid behind my legs and gave a little yelp as I reached for the door knob. "What is it, boy?" I gave Scooter a reassuring pat on the head and opened the door.

"Ta-da!" Mom shouted as the door swung open. Dad was standing in one spot, frozen, with his mouth hanging wide open.

I followed his gaze until I saw what my mom had unveiled. My brain couldn't figure out what I was seeing. Scooter had the right idea. He dropped his tail between his legs and went running out of the room.

CHAPTER 2

"**M**om?" I WHISPERED, NOT TAKING MY EYES OFF WHAT I was looking at.

"Wait! Start over! I'm going to turn on the voice recognition and recording feature. I want him to sound as life-like as you." Mom pressed a few buttons and smiled. "Okay, now what did you want to ask?"

I was staring at myself, but it wasn't me. The creature, or android, or robot, or whatever it was looked exactly like me. Same height, same eyes, same hair.

"Wh-what is it?"

Mom smiled and rubbed her hands together, "This is C-Y-R-S! Closed-loop Young Robot System—Cyrus!"

"Is it . . . alive?" I stuttered as the robot opened his eyes, blinked, and started turning his head from side to side, like he'd just woken up from a long nap.

Mom kept on talking. "See, we've been working on trying to replicate the human body and make the system look as real as possible. We went through hundreds of prototypes before we came up with Cyrus. Smith and Company thinks we can perfect the rest of the system by the end of the year! This will be ground breaking! Earth shattering! The news will *rock* the robotics community. No one has gotten this close! Do you know what this means, Shawn?"

"You made me into a robot?" I stepped forward and the robot was watching me. I waved my hand slowly and it mimicked my movement. I tugged on my ear and it did the same. It was like looking into a mirror.

My mom watched me and Cyrus. She let out a loud laugh and clapped her hands. "No! It means that artificial intelligence will be commonplace in just a few short years. Everyone will have access to it. We'll save lives with this research! I can't believe I'm part of such an important project."

"But dear," Dad finally spoke, "why does *this* one look like Shawn?"

Mom shrugged. She was annoyed that we cared so much about what he looked like and not about what he was capable of. "I spent so much time working on the processing boards and the programming, that I didn't put much thought into the outside. Before I brought him home he had to look human, so I showed the artist a family photo and she made a skin-like covering to look like Shawn. Neat, huh?"

I shook my head and started to back away when the robot copied me again. "No, that is not neat. That is super creepy. What are we supposed to do with a robotic me? Why is it here?"

Mom leaned forward and lowered her voice, "We're calling him a *he*, not an *it*." Then she raised her voice and looked over at the robot. "Cyrus, why don't you tell them why you're here."

Cyrus blinked slowly and then said, "I am here to integrate with the Cole family. Dr. Cole, her husband Mr. Nathaniel Cole, and their son Shawn Cole will demonstrate how to have realistic human interactions and relationships. I will study human emotions and try to replicate feelings. I will even learn to accept the family canine, basset hound, Scooter, as a close companion."

Dad looked over at me, "At least it, er, *he* doesn't sound like you."

"Oh! I can fix that," Mom lifted the back of Cyrus's shirt and flipped out a full-sized keyboard. "Okay, now he's programmed to sound like an eleven-year-old boy. Care to try that again, Cyrus?"

Cyrus's shoulders dropped a little and he wasn't standing up so straight. "I'm here to join the fam! I can't wait to learn all about how to be the best son and brother I can be. Oh! And I can't wait to give Scooter belly rubs!"

I heard Scooter whimper from the living room and laughed. "Well, that's cool. I always wanted a brother. Where's he sleeping?" I asked.

"I thought he could share your room for a while, and then we'll move him into the guest room." Mom looked at Dad, who shrugged.

"My room?" I asked. "No way!"

My mom moved forward and wrapped an arm around my shoulder, "Please, honey. You'll barely even know he's here. He'll be observing and keeping digital logs in order to integrate the information into his code. He can actually learn!"

"Fine," I crossed my arms, "but he better not touch my stuff!"

Cyrus woke me up four times that night.

First it was because his internal sensors overheated and a warning siren came on. I jumped out of bed when the alarm started. Scooter started howling. Mom and Dad came running into the room. Cyrus explained what was happening to my mom and she was able to make it stop with a few keystrokes.

At midnight, Cyrus's Wi-Fi signal, which had been set to the lab's secure server, couldn't connect to our server at our house.

"Shawn." I felt Cyrus poking me and rolled away from him. I covered my head with my pillow. "Shawn, Shawn, Shawn, Shawn."

"What?" I finally yelled. I knew he'd be able to repeat my name over and over until forever. Call me weak, but I gave in early.

"Do you know what the password is?" He pointed to one hand, which had a mini tablet built into it.

"Password for what?" I rubbed my eyes as they focused on the screen. "Can you play games on that thing?"

"Yes and password for the network. I need to login and upload data."

I pointed toward the door. "It's on the bottom of the cable box downstairs."

He left the room and I fell back to sleep right away.

An hour later Scooter woke me up, but it was Cyrus's fault. Scooter was barking and howling and panting so heavily he could barely catch his breath.

"Scoot? What's wrong?" I sat up and looked over to see Cyrus kneeling on the floor on all fours, snarling and growling at Scooter. He sounded like a real dog. "What are you doing?"

"Play bowing. It's how dogs interact," Cyrus explained and kept on barking at Scooter.

"Yes, it's how *dogs* interact. Not humans and dogs. Leave Scooter alone and go to bed, please. I'm so tired."

Cyrus went back to the cot and Scooter finally stopped wheezing.

The last time I woke up because Cyrus was standing next to my bed bouncing my autographed Los Angeles Lakers basketball. Nobody was allowed to bounce that ball. I snatched it away from him.

"Mom," I called down the hall. "He's touching my stuff!"

CHAPTER 3

I STARED AT THE PAPER ON MY DESK FOR WHAT SEEMED LIKE forever. *Okay Shawn*, I thought to myself. *You can do this. You know how to divide fractions. You learned this last week.*

"Mr. Cole?"

I looked up to the front of the classroom and saw Mr. Velazquez staring at me. I grabbed my pencil and started writing my name at the top of the pop quiz.

Mr. Velazquez cleared his throat and walked toward me. I figured if I kept my head down and my pencil busy, he'd walk right by and not notice I was too tired to see my hand in front of my face. I'd spent the first part of class taking a little power nap. Luckily, sleeping while sitting up with my eyes open was a unique skill of mine. It had come in handy during dinners when Dad went on and on about mergers and acquisitions or when Grandma Jill wanted me to watch hours of cat videos on her computer.

"Shawn?" my math teacher stopped right beside me and stared down. He lowered his glasses on his nose and said, "Or should I call you Shaw?"

"Huh?"

He pointed to my name, which I clearly hadn't finished writing, and then scanned the rest of the blank page. "The bell rang two minutes ago."

My eyes darted around the room. "Oh," I laughed nervously. "I didn't even notice. I'm really tired today. You see, my mom . . . " But what could I say? My mom brought home a twin brother robot who kept me up all night downloading MP3s, playing with my dog, and practicing his free throw?

Mr. Velazquez held out his hand, "I don't want to hear it, Shawn." I exhaled. *That* was a relief. I started to get up when he continued.

"A zero on a quiz is not going to help your average in this class. And you and I both know what that means about basketball." Mr. Velazquez was not only my math and science teacher, but he was also my basketball coach.

"Sir, I'll do better next time. I promise!" I was eyeing the clock, because I didn't want to be late for my next class.

He placed a pile of papers on my desk. "I'm glad to hear you say that, son, because next time is now. You'll need to do this makeup work tonight and have it on my desk tomorrow before class or . . . ?"

I lowered my head, "Or I'm benched."

"No," he replied.

"No? Well that's a relief," I said, gathering up the extra work.

"No, you won't be benched. You'll be off the team." He raised an eyebrow, like he knew what he'd just said had shocked me. "Now, get to class. You don't want to keep Mrs. Cray waiting."

I started toward the door.

"Oh, and Shawn?"

I looked back over my shoulder, "Yes?"

"Try to stay awake in her class, okay?"

———

When I got home after school I went into the kitchen for a snack. Cyrus was sitting at the table using a finger as a stylus, drawing on his tablet hand. Scooter, who was sprawled out on the tile floor, barely acknowledged my presence.

"Hi, Shawn. How was school?" Cyrus looked up for just a second before going back to whatever he was doing.

"It was horrible. Thanks for asking." I bit into an apple and chewed loudly, trying to annoy Cyrus. When that didn't work I asked, "Do you want to know why?"

"Yes," he nodded, but didn't look at me.

I looked over his shoulder to see what was so interesting. "Are you playing Total Pizza Calamity?"

"Mmmhmm."

I leaned in more, "But how? It's not out for another month."

"Well first, I downloaded the code for the old game. Then I ran background searches for codes matching—"

I held up my hand. "I didn't really need to know the specifics. When's my turn?" I looked over at my backpack and was reminded of the hours of work ahead of me.

Cyrus shrugged like he wasn't going to let me play, so I grabbed my bag prepared to storm out of the room. But then an idea crept into my head. I had all this extra work because of Cyrus. So why should *I* be punished for that? I turned on my heels, "Hey Cyrus, are you going to spend all day at the house? Or is Mom signing you up for school?"

He was still so interested in the quest to capture the head zombie pizza chef that he didn't look up. "Tomorrow. I start tomorrow."

"Oh," I tried to play it cool. "I think you'll like math class. What do you know about fractions?"

Cyrus dropped his hand and finally looked at me. I could see his eyes widen as his brain searched all available databases for information about fractions. He was about to open his mouth and spew out way more information than I'd ever need about denominators, so I tossed my stack of extra work from Mr. Velazquez in front of him.

"How about you work on that while I play for a bit. Then we'll switch?" Cyrus followed me into the living room, where I ran a cable from the tablet built into his palm to my game system. Scooter jumped up on the couch between the two of us. He seemed perfectly at home with the robot.

Before I'd even customized my character, Cyrus said, "I'm done. Let's start the two-player version."

I looked up surprised, "Did you double check your work?"

"I didn't need to. Fifth grade math isn't rocket science. Is it Scooter?" Cyrus scratched behind Scooter's ears, prompting a howl of delight.

"Traitor," I whispered to Scooter, who looked at me without an ounce of remorse in his bulging eyes and then turned back to Cyrus. Before starting the game, I flipped through the pages of math work. Every single problem was done. He'd even shown his work in the right places. "So you're a math genius, huh?"

"No, Shawn. I'm a robot. It's what we do."

"It's what we do," I mimicked.

"Did I do something to make you angry?" Cyrus asked.

"No," I shook my head. "But let me show you what humans do!" I got my character to sneak up on Cyrus's and steal his pizza-making ingredients. But Cyrus didn't fall for it. And an hour later, when my dad got home, Cyrus had defeated me on five consecutive levels.

"So, what was it that humans do?" Cyrus asked. I couldn't be sure, but I thought I detected a hint of sarcasm in his voice.

I threw down the controller and walked to the door. "That game is lame. I'm going over to James's house."

"Can I come?" Cyrus asked standing up, ready to follow me.

I shook my head, "No. I don't even know how to start explaining you to my friends. Besides, don't you have things to do? Important robot data transfers or something?"

Cyrus looked down at his feet and then at the dancing pepperonis on the TV screen. "Oh, yeah.

I guess so." He looked hurt, but I was probably just imagining things. He couldn't feel anything, like emotionally, yet. That's why he was living with us—to learn all that stuff.

I shut the door behind me, relieved to be away from the house. Who knew having a brother would make things so competitive? At least I'd gotten something from him, though. I was sure I'd ace that extra math work.

CHAPTER 4

MOM AND CYRUS WERE UP LATE WORKING IN HER OFFICE, so Cyrus spent the night on the couch. I think it was my mom's way of apologizing to me for the night before.

When I woke I felt like a new me. I slept well, and even dreamed of making the winning shot in the game against Westfield next week. My homework was done. I double checked that my name was spelled correctly as I tucked it into my backpack, then headed downstairs for breakfast.

Cyrus was sitting at the table wearing a navy blue polo shirt and khaki pants. Scooter was following my dad around as he served up bacon and eggs.

"Nice outfit, Cyrus," I said. "Looks like you're ready for school." I grabbed a piece of bacon and shoved it in my mouth. I might have elbowed Cyrus a little on the way past. He didn't respond, just looked at me out of the corner of his eyes.

My mom smiled. "Doesn't Cyrus look handsome!"

I held my glass of orange juice halfway up to my mouth. "I dress like that every day and you never say anything about me."

Mom nodded proudly and smoothed her hand over Cyrus's hair. "You *both* look handsome. This is a big step in the right direction. Cyrus will gather a lot of social and emotional data being around so many new people."

"Dr. Cole—" Cyrus started.

"Cyrus," Mom answered in a sing-songy voice. "Call me 'Mom'."

"Mom—" Cyrus started again. He sounded annoyed. "I could gather even more important social and emotional data around adults, people who are gainfully employed, intelligent, and evolved." He turned around in his chair and looked at my dad, "Like at Mr. Cole's work."

Dad raised an eyebrow and kept whisking the eggs. "Oh no! It's not Bring Your Fake Son to Work Day."

"Nathaniel!" Mom scolded. "Cyrus, honey—"

I choked on my orange juice. *Honey?*

I didn't say anything when I saw the look she was giving me. She continued, "We're just starting you out at school. It's a good experience to test your systems. We'll move you into new environments once everything is ready and calibrated. Think of it like baseline testing. This is as low as you'll go."

I dropped my fork. "What's that supposed to mean?"

Cyrus smirked at me, "It means that elementary school is beneath me."

I reached across the table and punched Cyrus in the shoulder. "You're a jerk," I said, grimacing as my knuckles bounced off Cyrus's metal body. That fake skin was very thin.

"Shawn Frederick Cole!" my mom yelled. "You lay another hand on Cyrus and you won't see the outside of your bedroom for the next fifteen years, or until you pay the lab back the multi-millions they've spent on your brother!"

"Whatever," I grunted as I grabbed my backpack. "Scooter, let's go!" Scooter always walked me down to the end of the driveway when I waited for the bus. But instead of getting up on his stubby legs and being a loyal best friend, he just lay next to Cyrus and looked up lovingly.

Cyrus smiled again. "See you at school, bro!" It felt like he was mocking me.

––––––––––

"Why are you in such a bad mood?" James asked as we walked into math class.

I looked around the room and frowned. I slunk into my seat and covered my head with the hood of my jacket. "You'll see."

"Uh . . . Shawn?" I felt James poking my shoulder. When I didn't respond he knocked on my head. "Yo, Shawn. You gotta see this. Your mom's here and there's another you."

I laid my head down on my desk and tried to hide in plain sight. After the second bell rang my mom explained to the class who Cyrus was and how we should treat him just like another student.

"So like, can he see through walls?"

My mom frowned. I don't think she was expecting questions like that when she offered to do a Question and Answer session about Cyrus, even though he was sitting right there in the room.

"No, that's not something we've programmed," Mom answered. "He is programmed to do everything that an eleven-year-old boy would do. He also can access information that most humans would need a computer to access. He can—"

"How smart is he, really?"

A smile spread across my mother's face. "Well, Cyrus has access to databases and search engines in one hundred seventy-five languages. He can retrieve data from journals and publications . . . " She could sense she was losing the other students' attention. "He's smart, really, really smart."

"Why does he look like Shawn?"

I could feel all my classmates' eyes burning holes into my back and I pulled my hood even tighter around my face.

"Because Shawn is the most handsome boy I know." Mom smiled at me.

Everyone in the class burst out laughing and I wished for invisibility or teleportation or anything that would get me out of this situation.

Luckily, Mr. Velazquez clapped his hands once. "All right, folks," he said. He pointed to the warm-up problems on the board and everyone got started as he walked my Mom to the door. He went back to his desk where he looked over the work I'd handed in the day before. I couldn't quite tell what he was thinking. His face didn't give anything away, so I hunched over my notebook and started my classwork.

"You know what?" Mr. Velazquez announced suddenly. "In honor of our new student, why don't we try something a little different today?"

The kids around me started chattering. I rolled my eyes, annoyed to be doing anything in honor of Cyrus.

"Let's see how well you've learned division of

fractions. Two of you will come up to the board and race to solve a problem. The winner will stay up and pick his or her next opponent. Let's start with Katrina and . . . " Mr. Velazquez looked around the room and then right at me, "Shawn."

I got up slowly and went to the board. As I approached my teacher leaned in and whispered, "Don't worry, Shawn, I'm going to give problems from your work the other night. You should be able to ace this." He winked and clapped me on the back. *Uh oh*, I thought, *he knows I didn't do that homework.*

"Okay, two-thirds divided by five-sixths."

Katrina started scribbling the problem on her side of the board, so I followed her lead. I could do this. I had to do this, especially with Cyrus watching. I didn't need the added humiliation. *Okay, flip the second fraction and cross multiply*, I reminded myself.

"Done!" Katrina called out.

"Nice job, Katrina. Who would you like to challenge?"

She smiled and pointed at Cyrus. "The robot, er, the new kid."

I hung my head in shame and headed back to my seat.

"Nice try, Shawn," Cyrus whispered as I walked by. He held out his hand for a high five but I brushed past him to my desk. I didn't need him feeling bad for me.

"And Cyrus for the win . . . " Mr. Velazquez announced for the tenth consecutive time. Cyrus had won every challenge and did the work in his head in a nanosecond each time. The class loved it. They clapped after each win. When the bell rang, all the girls asked Cyrus where his next class was and offered to walk him there.

"Shawn?" Mr. Velazquez stopped me on my way out. "This isn't your work." He pointed to the papers. "I was pretty sure when I first saw it, but now that I see your broth—" he paused, "Cyrus the robot, in action, I know he did your homework."

I bit my lip and hung my head.

"Cheating is a serious offense. I'll be reporting you to the principal," Mr. Velazquez frowned. "And, I'm sorry to have to do this, you're a great player, but you're off the basketball team."

I nodded. I felt like I wanted to punch something. Instead I just balled my hands into fists and squeezed until my fingers went numb. I watched as Cyrus laughed and talked to all the other kids in class and I wanted to hate him. But I knew it wasn't really him I was mad at, it was myself.

At lunch I watched as Cyrus sat with James and a bunch of the other guys from the team. I picked at my sandwich and mumbled to myself.

Two girls stopped in front of my table, blocking my view. "Shawn, your robot is *so* funny."

"You're supposed to call him Cyrus," the other girl said.

"Right. Your brother Cyrus is just so great. You're so lucky to have him around!" They nodded at each other and then walked away.

I closed my eyes and pretended I wasn't in the lunchroom. I tried to think of some place I'd rather be. The beach, maybe. But I hated sand in my toes. An amusement park would be okay, except that I was afraid of heights.

"Hey, can I sit with you?" Cyrus's voice made me open my eyes.

"Why?" I asked, shoving my sandwich back inside my lunch bag.

"To be honest," Cyrus leaned forward, "I wanted to get away from those guys." He pointed back over his shoulder at the guys on the team. "I don't know how you do it every day. One of them is actually drinking his milk through a straw up his nose."

I smiled. "That would be Jensen."

"So, did you get kicked off the team?"

"How did you kn—?"

Cyrus held up his hand and said, "I ran calculations on the possibilities."

I nodded. "Of course you did. Mom and Dad are going to freak when they find out I cheated."

Cyrus rubbed his hands together like he was hatching a plan. "What if I helped get you back on the team?" he asked.

"Why would you do that?"

"Call it a special project. I beat Total Pizza Calamity. I need something else to do with my time. Besides, you're my brother and according to my research, brothers are supposed to help brothers. After today, I have a new appreciation for what it's like to be a twelve-year-old boy."

I thought about his offer. It just didn't make sense. I've been acting like such a jerk to him. "So, you want to help me get back on the team, even though I've been kind of—"

"Mean, rude, abrasive, jealous?" Cyrus smiled. "Math isn't my only specialty. I'm good at English, too."

I laughed. "Yes, all of those things, but you still want to do something nice for me?"

Cyrus nodded. "Like I said, if the research says brothers help each other out, then that's what I need to do to learn to be your brother. I think it might be fun."

I leaned forward. "So, do you have a plan?"

Cyrus's mouth broke into a wide grin and he said, "You're going to love it!"

CHAPTER 5

THE ENTIRE BUS RIDE HOME, I KEPT WONDERING WHAT WAS going on with Cyrus. He'd stayed after school for mid-season basketball try-outs. He knew he'd have no problem getting Coach's attention, because he couldn't miss. He actually programmed an app to install in his arms to make sure the ball went in every single time.

From there he was supposed to give the coach a sob story about life as a robot and how he was trying to adjust. He'd tell Coach that he asked to do my homework for me, so that he could feel like a real boy. Coach Velazquez was a sensitive guy, I was sure this plan would work.

After I closed the front door behind me, I tried to tiptoe upstairs. I wanted to wait in my room until Cyrus got home so I knew for sure the plan went as expected. I made it halfway up before hitting the squeaky step by accident.

"Shawn?" My dad came through the kitchen door into the living room. "I thought I heard you come in."

"I was just going to get started on my homework." I couldn't look at him.

Dad sat on the couch and patted the cushion beside him and said, "Come have a seat." His tone was neutral. He didn't seem angry.

When I sat down, I let my backpack slide off my shoulder and onto the floor. Scooter came over to sniff around and see if I'd left any snacks in my lunch bag.

When he smelled my half-eaten sandwich, he started pawing at the zipper.

"I just received a call from Coach Velazquez," my dad started to say, and he raised an eyebrow at me.

This was not the plan. Maybe Coach had called before Cyrus could work his charm. I bit my lip and debated what to do. One on hand, I could deny everything, get caught in a lie and wind up grounded for years. One the other hand, I could admit to what I'd done and *still* get grounded for years. "Dad, let me explain, okay? See I didn't want to get kicked off the team, so I sort of tricked Cyrus into helping me and then Coach found out and—"

"Shawn, what are you talking about? What do you mean 'get kicked off the team'?" Dad was looking at me suspiciously. His eyes were closed a little and his upper lip was twitching the way it did before he started in on a lecture.

"Because I cheated on my homework. That's why Coach called, right?" There, I'd admitted to it.

My dad stood up. "You did what?" My dad's voice turned from calm discussion to angry roar. "Your coach called to say Cyrus tried out for basketball, but didn't make the team. The coach thought we should know before Cyrus got home so we could help him make sense of things. He didn't mention anything about cheating."

Cyrus didn't make the team. How was that possible? Coach didn't tell Dad about the homework. Cyrus's plan must have worked; Coach must want me back on the team! I couldn't help but smile until I saw the look on Dad's face. "Oh, huh," I laughed nervously. "Yeah . . . I'll just go to my room now."

Dad nodded angrily, "We'll discuss this with your mother when she gets home. Until then, consider yourself grounded until further notice."

I heard the muffled conversations downstairs when Mom and Cyrus got home. I heard my Dad's voice getting louder and louder. I sat on my bed and tossed my basketball up in the air over and over. I tried to look through my homework, but I couldn't concentrate.

There was a scratching at my door, so I got up to let Scooter in. At least I'd have some company while I waited to hear how much trouble I was in.

"Hey, thought you might be hungry," Cyrus said. He held out a plate with meatloaf, mashed potatoes, and broccoli. Scooter was sitting at his feet, hoping a scrap would fall off the plate.

"Thanks," I said, taking it from him and letting them both in. I sat on my bed and picked at the meatloaf.

"So you told your dad about the homework?" Cyrus sat at my desk.

I nodded.

"Well, that was stupid. Now you're in trouble,"

Cyrus said looking through the pages of the math book on my desk.

I rolled my eyes. "I thought they were going to find out anyway. Dad said Coach called and I freaked out. I didn't know your plan had worked."

Cyrus replied sheepishly, "It didn't."

"What do you mean?" I looked up from the plate and dropped a piece of broccoli. Scooter sniffed it twice and turned his nose up at it.

"I asked to try out for the team, and I told the coach how you'd been helping me so much at home and that I did your homework to help repay you. He thinks you're a good kid. But you're not back on the team. Coach Velasquez knew exactly what I was trying to do."

"So, I'm not on the team, but you're not on the team, either?" I was actually relieved. I'd spent the last few days being so competitive with Cyrus that if he'd made the team I would have been really mad.

"I'm not on the team, either," Cyrus repeated.

"Why not?"

"I missed all the shots."

"You did?" I was surprised. Cyrus had programmed himself to be perfect at basketball.

"On purpose, of course. I don't really like basketball. All that running back and forth in such a small space doesn't make sense. I guess sports just aren't my thing. I also realized if I made the team I'd have to spend a lot of time with the other guys. I know they're your friends, Shawn, but they are weird and disgusting."

I laughed and thought about flinging some mashed potatoes at him, but decided I was already in enough trouble with Mom and Dad. "But why didn't Coach tell Dad about the homework?"

Cyrus shrugged. "He probably emailed."

I considered that. "This whole thing was so stupid.

I should have just done my own work and not tricked you into doing it. Thanks for trying to help me out."

Cyrus nodded and said, "It's nothing. After today I have a greater appreciation for what you have to deal with every day. Human kids are not my favorite things in the world."

I laughed. "But you were Mr. Popularity today. The girls were following you around, batting their eyelashes, like 'Oh, Cyrus, you're so smart.' And the guys thought you were cool. So, why is that so bad?"

"Because everyone wanted something from me. They liked me only to get something for themselves. It made me feel confused. My emotional programming is not sophisticated enough to know who my real friends are and who is using me for their own gain." Cyrus's face scrunched up like he was thinking about something, which I'd learned was his *searching available databases* face. "It's too bad humans can't be more like dogs."

Scooters ears perked up.

Cyrus continued, "I know why Scooter likes me—treats and belly rubs. I don't know why humans like me or why they like each other, even."

I nodded, "I get it. So you're not, like, street smart. You're book smart."

"Actually, I know a lot about streets. For instance did you know that Lombard Street in San Francisco is the curviest street in the world with eight sharp turns in just one block? And—"

I stuck a finger in each ear and groaned. Cyrus's mouth kept right on moving. I shoved my head under the pillow and sang loudly trying to get him to stop. At that point I was actually hoping my parents were ready to come upstairs and let me know my punishment. It would be less painful than hearing Cyrus's fact database.

"Okay . . . okay," he shouted above my singing. "I know when I'm not wanted."

I rolled over and smiled. "Hey, Cyrus, thanks again for trying to help me out today."

"Sorry it didn't work," Cyrus said as he opened my door to let himself out.

"Yeah, me too. Do you think you could hypnotize Coach Velazquez into letting me back in the team? Do you have any way to learn mind control?" I raised an eyebrow.

Cyrus tapped a finger to his temple. "I'll get working on that, Shawn. But until then, I *can* help you with fractions. Not by doing the work for you, but by helping you learn it yourself."

I considered his offer. It seemed like something a brother would do. "Yeah, man. That would be awesome!" I walked over to my desk and pointed at my textbook. "Could we start now? I mean, I've got nowhere to be for the next few years or so."